The Ogress and the Snake

For the storytellers of Somalia

First published in Great Britain and the USA in 2009 by
Frances Lincoln Children's Books, 4 Torriano Mews,
Torriano Avenue, London NW5 2RZ.
www.franceslincoln.com

British Library Cataloguing in Publication Data available on request

ISBN 978-1-84507-870-6

Set in Bembo

Printed in the UK by CPI Bookmarque, Croydon, CR0 4TD

1 3 5 7 9 8 6 4 2

The Ogress and the Snake
and other Stories from Somalia

Retold by Elizabeth Laird

Illustrations by Shelley Fowles

F

FRANCES LINCOLN
CHILDREN'S BOOKS

Acknowledgements

It was thanks to the British Council – and in particular to
Michael Sargent, the Director of Addis Ababa at the time –
that this story-collecting project happened. In Jigjiga, everything
was arranged by Osman Abdulahi Ahmed, Head of the Culture
Department (who told me the story of Hirsi and Kabaalaf).
The arduous work of finding the storytellers and translating
the stories was done by Moge Abdi Omer, the team leader in
Culture at the Department of Education and Culture Bureau.
And I'd never have got to Jigjiga at all if hadn't been for
Teklehaimanot Yigletu, my courageous driver, who braved
the bad roads and the bandits to get me to the storytellers.
I want to thank them all.

Contents

Introduction

I first went to Somalia forty years ago. Travelling over a vast plain, I saw a little family of nomads with their three camels. The father in front led the first camel. Behind him walked his wife, while a toddler straggled along behind with a few goats. A kettle hung from one the camels' necks. The family's home, a hut of poles and matting, had been piled on the back of the second camel, while a few bed rolls and saddle bags were carried by the third. Where had this family come from? Where were they going in that vast emptiness? They waved to us cheerfully as we passed, and walked on.

At Berbera, a town on the Red Sea coast, I looked down white painted alleyways towards the flashing blue of the sea. Old sailing ships, the dhows of India and Arabia, were bobbing at anchor in the port. I half expected to see Sinbad the sailor hauling in his anchor. Instead, I saw clouds of dust approaching as herdsmen, whirling their sticks above their heads, drove their cattle down to the sea to be shipped across to Yemen.

I was lucky to visit Somalia when I did. For many years now it has been a dangerous and tragic place. Droughts have brought starvation. Lawlessness and civil war have killed thousands. I couldn't have gone there again. But thirty years after my first visit I went to the Somali region of Ethiopia, where many Somali people live. The main town there is called Jigjiga. Bandits sometimes attacked travellers on the roads, and my heart pounded as we drove through the deserted hill passes above the small city. But we arrived safely, and I spent happy days in Jigjiga collecting stories, some of which appear in this book.

Many different people told them to me. There was Abdul Hakim Abdulahi Jibril, a teacher, who told me *How the Cat became Woman's Friend* and *How the Dog became Man's Friend*. We sat in the grounds of a Koranic school under the shade of a tree, and all the children crowded round to listen. Then there was elderly Professor Ahmed Mohammed Ali, who told me *The Sun and the Raven* and *The Miraculous Head* as night fell outside the windows of his office. On one memorable evening, I was entertained in the home of Hukun Hussein Fura. She brewed for me her own delicious coffee, and burned incense till clouds of it filled the room, while her little daughter Ikran told me the story of *The Ogress and the Snake*. *Deya Ali and the Thieves* was narrated by Aisha Awadem as she sat among a group of her fellow midwives. *The Good Prince* was told to me by Abdulrahman Abdulahi, a cloth merchant in the ancient walled city of Harar. We sat on magnificent carpets in the old Emir's palace as the tale slowly unfolded.

Before each story began, the narrator would recite a little verse, to get everyone in the mood. Then, when the story had finished, everyone would say, "What does it all mean?" and a great discussion would break out.

Elizabeth Laird

Can you see what I see?
Can you hear what I hear?
No! What can you see?
What do you hear?
Tell us!

Traditional saying used to introduce a Somali story

The Ogress and the Snake

In the land of Somalia, there lived a man and his wife who had five little daughters. Their house stood on the edge of the wild, dry bush. It was a hard life for the girls' parents. The father had to take his sheep far away to find grazing for them, and their mother had to work from morning until night to keep the family clothed and fed.

One sad day, the children's mother fell ill and died. The family was plunged into sorrow. The girls tried to do everything on their own, but they were too small to carry the heavy water jars home from the spring, and they didn't know how to cook and clean the house.

For a while they managed as best they could, but one day their father came home with a strange woman at his side.

"Children," he said, "this is my new wife. She's your mother now."

The new wife was beautiful, but there was no smile in her eyes. She looked coldly at the children and shook them off when they tried to hug her.

That night, when the five sisters went to bed, the oldest one heard her stepmother say to her husband, "How ugly your children are! And what bad manners they have."

"My love," murmured her husband. "Surely…" but his wife had turned away and wasn't listening.

In the morning, the big sister gathered the little ones round her.

"Try to be good," she whispered to them. "We must make our new mother love us."

But the next night, she heard her stepmother talking again.

"I won't look after these lazy, dirty girls," she was saying. "Do you expect me to be their slave?"

"Have patience, my dear," said her husband. "You'll learn to love them in time."

But the stepmother didn't learn to love the five little girls. She hated them more and more. She was careful, now, to speak to her husband only when none of the children could hear, and every night she said the same thing.

"You must choose," she told him. "If you want me to stay, these bad girls must go. Take them into the bush and leave them there."

"But, my darling, think of the wild animals! The lions and hyenas! They'd be torn to pieces. No, no, I could never abandon my children."

But his wife persisted, night after night, and at last her husband began to weaken.

"I'll take the older girls, if I must," he said, "but not the little one. Not my baby."

"All of them," his wife answered firmly. "I don't want to see their greedy faces ever again."

The next morning, with a heavy heart, the girls' father woke the children early.

"Come, get up," he said. "We're going on a journey."

"A journey? Where to?" they asked eagerly.

"Are we going where Mother is?" said the little one, winding her arms around her father's neck.

He lifted her on to his camel and led it out into the scratchy, dusty bush, with the others trotting along behind.

They walked all day. The hot sand blistered their feet and their mouths grew dry with thirst. At last they all began to cry.

"Take us home, Father," they sobbed. "We want to go home!"

Their father stopped, lifted the smallest child down from the camel's back and tied it to a nearby tree.

"It's too far," he told them. "We'll sleep here, and go back tomorrow."

The children looked round fearfully. The sun was setting and long grey shadows with pointed fingers were spreading across the land.

"What if a lion comes?" whispered one of them.

"Or a leopard?" breathed another.

"Or a hyena?" wailed a third.

Their father couldn't bear to look at them.

"Don't be afraid," he said. "Lie down and sleep. I'll be nearby, with the camel. You'll hear him grunting in the night, and know I'm not far away."

Trustingly, the girls lay down under a tree, and were soon fast asleep.

The smallest sister woke first in the morning. She shook the oldest one awake.

"I'm hungry and thirsty," she said, "and I want my daddy."

The oldest sister put her arms round her.

"He's near us, with the camel," she said. "Can't you hear it grunting?"

"That's not our camel," another sister told her. "It's a wild one. Look."

All the sisters jumped up and looked round. Their father and his camel were nowhere to be seen, and a herd of wild camels was grazing on the thorn bushes nearby. The girls trembled with fear.

"Father!" they called out as loudly as they could. "Where are you?" Together they began to sing:

Father, your children
are lost and alone.
Come and find us,
and take us home!

But the only answer was a rustle of wind in the leaves, and the croak of a vulture who was watching them from a rock nearby.

All that day, the sisters hunted for their father, stumbling about on the stony ground. But when the shadows of evening began to lengthen again, the oldest one called the others to her.

"Father's not coming back," she told them. "We're alone now. We must find someone to help us before we die of hunger."

The second sister tugged at her ragged sleeve.

"Here comes someone. Look there," she said.

A cloud of dust was rolling along the ground towards them. From inside it came the tinkle of bells and the tap of sharp little hooves on the hard dry ground. As the cloud came nearer, the girls saw a flock of goats and sheep, and a shepherd girl driving them along from behind.

The oldest sister went up to her.

"Please," she said. "You must help us. My sisters and I are lost out here, and we're dying of hunger and thirst. If we have to stay out in the open for another night, the wild animals will get us for sure."

The shepherd girl lifted her stick and drove her little flock on.

"Find someone else," she called back. "I can't help you."

The oldest sister ran after her.

"There is no one else," she panted. "If you don't help us, we'll die!"

The shepherd girl stopped walking and looked at her sadly.

"I'd like to help you," she said. "But I can't take you home with me. My mother's name is Degder. She eats people. She'd gobble you up, every last one of you."

The oldest sister stepped back in horror.

"Degder the Ogress?" she gasped.

She was about to turn away, but then, from the hills nearby, came the *whoop! whoop!* of a hyena.

"Please hide us!" she begged. "Just give us a place to shelter in, a bite of food and a little water to drink. We'll be as quiet as mice. Your mother won't even know we're there."

She pleaded with the ogress's daughter for a long time, until at last the girl gave in.

"I'll do my best for you," she said. "You look so sad and lonely. Hide in the cloud of dust that my sheep and goats are kicking up, and follow them when they run through the hole in the thorn fence into their pen. Sleep there, inside the pen, but stay near the entrance. If my mother finds you, you must run away. She's fast, but you might have a chance."

So the five sisters hid in the cloud of dust and followed the shepherd girl home. They bolted through the hole in the fence with the sheep and goats, and sat there, trembling with fright.

★★★

Degder the Ogress was waiting for her daughter.

"My darling, my beauty, you're home at last," she cried. Then she chanted:

Fetch my water!
Sweep the floor!
Light the fire
and shut the…

She stopped suddenly, lifted her nose and sniffed the air.

"People! I smell people!" she growled, looking towards the pen where the sheep and goats were settling down to sleep.

Catch them!
Hook them!
Kill them!
Cook them!

The shepherd girl tried to lead her mother back to the house.

"There's no one here except me," she said. "You surely wouldn't eat me, Mother dear?"

The Ogress stared at her with her big red eyes.

"Eat my darling? Eat my beauty? No, but

I'm hungry! I'll kill a sheep, I'll kill a goat and eat them for my supper."

And she began to run towards the pen.

The little girls heard her coming and clutched each other, their hearts beating wildly.

"No, no, Mother!" cried Degder's daughter. "You're tired. You need a rest. Come, lie down. I'll make your supper. I'll bring you a drink." And with soft, gentle words she led her mother back inside and shut the door.

Degder sank down beside the fire, shaking her big ugly head from side to side.

"I'm sick!" she moaned. "My ear aches.

It needs fat, hot fat
from the sheep's thick tail.
Boil it up, good and hot.
Pour it in from the pot.
Quick! Quick!"

The daughter did as she was told, boiling up a pot of fat. "In your ear, Mother?" she said doubtfully. "But surely it will burn you?"

"The ache! The ache!" cried the Ogress. "Pour it in. Now! Now!"

So the Ogress's daughter poured the panful of boiling fat into her mother's ear, and it ran straight into her brain, and she fell down dead, right there on the floor.

The children hiding in the sheep pen heard Degder's daughter scream, and they ran to see what had happened.

"My mother's dead," the girl was wailing. "She was cruel and wicked, but she loved me, and now I'm alone in the world."

The oldest sister put her arms round her.

"You're not alone," she said. "Let us live with you here and be your new family. We're six sisters now, instead of five."

Everyone from miles around was relieved to hear that Degder the Ogress was dead. They came to her house, and danced and sang outside it.

The wicked Ogress spoiled our lives.
She ate our children and our wives.
We were her meat, we were her bread,
now we are happy, for Degder is dead!

★★★

The girls lived happily together, until one day Degder's daughter told the others that she was leaving home to be married.

"You must manage on your own now," she said. "But you may stay in my house. I'm giving it to you."

The oldest sister tossed and turned all night, wondering how they would make their living. When the sun rose, she woke the others.

"Fetch wood and water and light the fire," she told them. "There's a little flour left in the jar. Bring it to me."

She worked hard, and soon made some bread.

"Take it to the market and sell it," she told the middle sisters.

It was a long way to market, but the girls ran fast, and when the sun was setting they came home with a little money in their pockets.

"It's not much, but it will do," the oldest sister said. "This is how we'll live from now on."

Time passed again. The sisters worked hard. The little ones fetched firewood and water from the river. The oldest one made bread. The middle ones took the bread to the market to sell. There was never enough money, and sometimes the children went to bed hungry, but they managed all the same.

The river was a long way from the house. Every day, the little ones had to walk miles, carrying heavy pots of water.

"Why can't we take water from the spring near our house?" they kept asking the oldest sister. "There's plenty there, and it looks clean and sweet."

But the oldest sister had seen a big snake in the water hole. It lay in the depths, coiling and uncoiling, waiting for a tender little girl to eat.

One hot day, the smallest sister set off for the river with the empty water pot on her head.

"It's so far to the river," she thought, "and I'm hot and tired."

She crept up to the water hole and looked in.

"I can't see the snake," she told herself. "He must have gone out hunting."

She dipped her pot into the water and began to fill it.

But the clever snake had been lurking in a dark corner all the time, waiting for its chance. It shot out and wrapped itself round the little girl's leg. Then it began to drag her down and down, into the water.

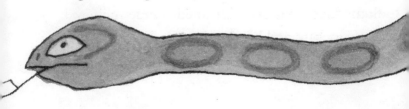

"Help!" screamed the smallest sister. "Help! The snake's trying to eat me!"

The others came running at once. They took hold of the little girl's arms and pulled. The snake was strong and hungry. It pulled too. The girls' arms were straining, and they were getting tired, but slowly they were winning.

Suddenly the snake gave up, and with an angry hiss slid back into the water. As it went down, it nudged the stones lying on the bottom of the water hole.

Something yellow gleamed and glittered. Something hard and bright.

The oldest sister caught sight of it.

"Gold!" she said to herself. "There's treasure down there!"

She picked up the youngest sister and carried her back to the house. She dried her and comforted her and gave her something to eat. But all the time, her thoughts were on the gold.

The next day, the oldest sister took a piece of meat and placed it by the water hole. Then she hid behind a bush and waited, a big knife in her hand.

The sun rose high. Flies buzzed round her head. But the oldest sister didn't move.

At last the snake smelled the meat. It lifted its head from the water and slowly, cautiously, slithered out of the hole. In a flash, the oldest sister pounced, and with one slash of her knife she cut off the snake's head. Then she jumped down into the water and began to pick up the gold. There was so much that she couldn't carry it all.

"Come and help me!" she called to the others. "We're rich! We're rich! We'll never be hungry again!"

Life was good for the girls from now on. They left the Ogress's little house, and built a fine big one for themselves. They bought cows and sheep too, and hired men to look after them.

One evening, the youngest sister was sitting outside the house, playing with her kitten. She wasn't a baby any longer, but a pretty young girl. Looking up, she saw a pair of beggars coming towards her. They wore rags, and had no shoes on their feet. Their eyes burned with hunger in their thin faces.

"Food, for the love of God!" the man was calling out. "Take pity! Help us!"

The little sister knew that voice.

"Father?" she said, jumping up. "Is it really you?"

The man stared at her for a long moment, then his face broke into a smile of wonder.

"My little girl! You're alive!"

The other sisters heard him and ran out of the house.

"Alive and well! All of you! Thank God! Thank God!" their father cried, opening his arms and trying to embrace them all at the same time.

His wife hung back, looking ashamed. The oldest

sister went up to her and took her hand.

"Come into the house, stepmother," she said. "You look tired and hungry. You're at home now, with us."

That evening, as they ate a delicious meal, the girls told the father of their adventures, and he told them all his troubles.

"I haven't known a moment's peace since I left you in the desert," he confessed. "Every day I cursed myself. And God has punished us. Our sheep and cattle all became sick and died. Thieves broke into our house and stole the little we had. And, worst of all, God gave us no more children. Now he has been merciful, and has led us to find you again. Please forgive us, dear children, for what we did."

The girls forgave their father and stepmother. They looked after them from then on, and the family lived together happily ever after.

How the Cat became Woman's Friend

In the beginning, when all the animals had just been created, the first cat came to drink at a pool. She looked down and saw her face in the water.

"I'm not like all the other animals," she said to herself. "They're big and strong, but I'm only little. I need a powerful friend to look after me."

Just then, the first antelope passed by. He had long sharp horns on his head and his tail flicked from side to side.

"The antelope can run faster than all the other animals," thought the cat. "He can run like the wind. He's the one to look after me."

So the cat and the antelope became friends. They played chasing and jumping games, and when the sun rose high in the sky, they rested together under a tree.

But one day, the first lion jumped out of the bushes and roared at them. The antelope's eyes opened wide. His legs trembled and his nose twitched with fright.

He jumped up and raced away across the plain until he was far, far away.

"Hmm," thought the cat. "The lion's stronger than the antelope. I'll make friends with him."

So the cat and the lion became friends. Every night they stalked and hunted together, and when they lay down to rest they purred in harmony.

But one day, the first elephant came by, with her baby at her side.

"That baby elephant looks good to eat," the lion told the cat. "I'm going to catch him."

The lion chased after the little elephant. The baby squealed with terror. His mother heard his cries. She trumpeted with rage, and rushed at the lion with her tusks. The lion raced away with a disappointed snarl, and disappeared in a whirl of dust over the crest of the hill.

"I see," thought the cat. "The lion is frightened of the elephant. Perhaps she'll be my friend."

So the cat and the elephant became friends. All day long they strolled across the wide plain and when night came the cat slept curled up against the elephant's great grey side.

But one day, the elephant lifted her trunk to sniff the air.

"I smell sugar cane," she said, "and I'm going to eat it."

She went down to the first man's field and began to eat the sugar cane, crunching it up in her great big teeth. The man heard her. He picked up his spear, and pulled a flaming stick out of the fire. He ran out of his hut and began to chase her, shouting with fury. The elephant ran away.

"Aha," thought the cat. "The man is stronger

than the elephant. I'll follow him."

The elephant ran on and on, and the man ran after her, his spear at the ready. For days and days they ran, up the hills and down the valleys, through the forest and across the plain.

"You've learned your lesson now," the man said. "You won't eat my sugar cane again."

He turned around and went home, and the cat followed him.

The first woman was waiting at the door of her hut. She was very angry.

"Where have you been all this time?" she scolded her husband. "The cow hasn't been milked, and the fence hasn't been mended, and the barley hasn't been sown in the field. You're a lazy, good-for-nothing fellow, and you won't get any supper tonight."

The cat was listening all this while.

"So that's it!" she thought. "The woman is stronger than the man. I'll make friends with her."

And the cat went up to the woman, and rubbed her back against the woman's leg, and curled her tail around it, and purred out loud. And she became the woman's friend for ever more.

How the Dog became
Man's Friend

The first man, Adam, was the father of us all. He lived in the Garden of Eden, where no danger could come near him and no evil could touch him. But Adam disobeyed God, and to punish him, God sent him out of the Garden of Eden and shut the great gates behind him.

In the wide world outside the garden lived all the animals. They stared at Adam curiously.

"Look at his legs," said the zebra. "They're strong and straight like mine. I'm sure he's a zebra like me."

"Legs like yours?" hooted the monkey. "Are you crazy? He's only got two, not four. Besides, there's not a stripe on his body. But look at his hands. They're just like mine. He's a monkey. I'm sure of it."

"A monkey? Then where's his tail?" scoffed the eagle. "Anyway, he's not hairy all over like you are. I can't tell from here, but I'm sure he's covered with feathers. Mark my words, he's a bird."

"Whoever saw a bird without a beak or wings?" hissed the snake. "His skin is smooth. I think he's a brother of mine."

"A snake with arms and legs?" laughed the hyena. "In my opinion…"

The lion held up a majestic paw. At once the animals fell silent and looked at him respectfully.

"There's only one way to find out for sure," he growled. "We must send a messenger to talk to him. Dog, you can run fast. Go to this strange creature and speak to him. Ask him if he wants to fight us, or live with us in peace."

The dog wagged his tail and bounded off happily. He liked to make new friends.

"Who are you?" he said to Adam. "All of us want to know. Are you a friend, or do you mean to harm us?"

Adam smiled at him.

"I'm Adam the man," he said, "and I'm a stranger in the world. I want to live with you in peace."

The dog barked joyfully, and, turning round, he raced back towards the other animals.

"Did you hear that?" the mouse said nervously. "The dog barked. The new creature must have threatened him." And she bolted to safety down her hole.

"He's running away as fast as he can," said the antelope, his long legs trembling under him. "Better safe than sorry." And away he dashed, over the hill.

The other animals smelled their fear. The baboon scrambled off up the high rocks. The elephant's baby caught hold of her mother's tail and ran away behind her. The vulture flapped up into the sky. The crocodile slid into the river. Soon, only the lion was left.

"*Wuff!* Stop! *Wuff!*" barked the dog. "Come back, all of you. He's a friend! A friend." But the lion thought he'd said, "It's the end! The end!" And with a sullen roar, he loped off to a distant cave.

Frantically, the dog ran one way and another, trying to reach the animals. "Stop!" he kept shouting. "Come back!" but none of them heard him. They stayed fearfully in their hiding-places.

Sadly, the dog returned to Adam. He lay down, panting, at Adam's feet.

"They wouldn't listen to me," he said sadly. "They're all afraid of you."

Adam was angry.

"If they won't be friends with me, then I'll be no friend to them," he said. "I'll hunt them with my spear. Stay with me, Dog, and help me."

So the dog stayed with the man, and hunted with him from that day on, and they became friends for ever more.

Deya Ali and the Thieves

Deya Ali the fox lived with her uncle, the lion. Six friends lived with them too – the hyena, the vulture, the bag of coffee beans, the forked stick, the butter gourd and the sack of barley chaff.

They all lived happily together, with their goats and their cows and their camels.

All except Deya Ali. She was jealous of her friends.

"There are too many of us here," she thought. "I have to share everything with everyone else. There's never enough for me."

One day, Deya Ali said to her uncle, the lion, "Uncle, when I take the cows and the goats to the fields tomorrow, send the hyena out with me."

"All right," said the lion.

So the next day, Deya Ali and the hyena took the cattle out together.

When it was nearly evening, Deya Ali said to the hyena, "I'm very hungry. If I don't eat something at once, I'm sure I'll faint."

"I'm hungry, too," said the hyena. "Let's eat one of the cows."

"Oh, we can't do that," said Deya Ali. "The lion will be angry with us. Look. There are some men down there, near the river. They have some nice fat cows. Why don't you kill one of them for us?"

So the hyena ran down to the river, and tried to kill a cow.

The men saw him and ran after him. The hyena was frightened, and he ran and ran, over the hills and far away.

"That's the end of him," thought Deya Ali.

She drove the cattle back to the village.

"Dear Uncle," she said to the lion. "I'm very tired. I've been looking after the cattle by myself, all on my own. That stupid hyena ran off after the men's cows and they chased him away. You won't see him again. And I have been working, working all day long."

"That's bad, niece," said the lion. "Come and rest."

The next day, the lion said to Deya Ali, "Who will help you today?"

Deya Ali thought for a moment.

"Send the vulture out with me," she said.

So off went Deya Ali and the vulture with all the cows and goats.

When they arrived at the meadow, Deya Ali said to the vulture, "Please, Vulture, I'm so hungry. You stay and look after the cattle. I'll look for some food. If I find something good, I'll bring it back for you."

The vulture agreed, so Deya Ali ran away. All day she looked for food, and she found all kinds of good things to eat.

In the evening, when the sun was going down, she came back to the vulture.

"Deya Ali, did you bring something for me?" said the vulture. "I'm so hungry."

"Yes, and it's very nice," said Deya Ali. "Open your mouth wide."

So the vulture opened her mouth and Deya Ali

put a big stone inside it. The vulture tried to swallow the stone, but it stuck in her throat.

The vulture tried to speak, but she couldn't. She could only call, "*Humu! Humu!*"

Deya Ali drove the cattle back to the village.

"Dear Uncle," she said. "I'm so tired. That stupid vulture went off early this morning to look for food. She's been stuffing herself all day. Her throat's so full now, she can't speak. All she can say is '*Humu! Humu!*' But I have been working and working all day long."

"Is this true?" the lion roared to the vulture.

"*Humu! Humu!*" the vulture said.

The lion was angry. He tried to beat the vulture.

She flapped up into the sky, and flew over the hills and far away.

"That's the end of her," thought Deya Ali. "Now the second one has gone."

The next morning, Deya Ali said to the lion, "Send the forked stick out with me today. He can help me guard the cattle."

So the forked stick and Deya Ali went out together. They looked after the cattle all day. When it was nearly time to go home, Deya Ali saw some farmers. They were cutting sticks to make a fence for their cattle.

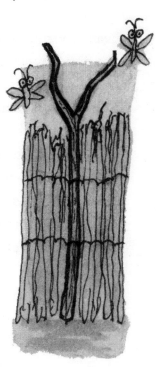

"Look," she said to the forked stick. "There are your uncles, the sticks. Why don't you go and greet them?"

"All right," said the forked stick, going to greet his uncles.

"Here's a nice stick," said the farmers, and they picked up the forked stick and tied him to the fence.

"That's the end of him," thought Deya Ali. "Now the third one has gone."

Deya Ali drove the cattle back to the village. She said to the lion, "That stupid forked stick ran to greet his uncles. The farmers caught him and tied him to the fence. And I've been guarding the cattle alone all day."

"My poor niece," said the lion. "You're tired. Come and rest."

The next morning, Deya Ali said to the lion, "Send the bag of coffee beans out with me today. He can help me guard the cattle."

So the next day, Deya Ali and the bag of coffee beans took the cattle out. In the afternoon, some travellers passed them on the road.

"Look at those people!" said Deya Ali. "They're hot and thirsty. They need a drink. Coffee beans, can you help them?"

"All right," said the bag of coffee beans, and he went up to the people.

"Look!" the people said. "Coffee beans! Let's boil some water and make ourselves coffee."

So they boiled some water, put the coffee beans in it and made themselves some coffee. Then they drank it.

"That's the end of the coffee beans," thought Deya Ali. "Now the fourth one has gone."

She drove the cattle back to the village, and said to her uncle, the lion, "That stupid bag of coffee beans went to speak to some thirsty travellers. They made a drink with him, and drank him up. But I have been working, guarding the cattle all day long."

"You must be very tired, then," said the lion. "Come and rest."

The next morning, Deya Ali said to her uncle, "Send the butter out with me today."

"All right," said the lion.

So the next morning, Deya Ali and the butter went out with the cattle together.

When the sun was high in the sky, Deya Ali said to the butter, "My poor butter, you look so tired. Sit on that stone and rest."

"Thank you, Deya Ali," said the butter, and she sat down on the stone.

But the stone was hot. At once, the butter melted and ran down, into the ground.

"That's the end of the butter," thought Deya Ali. "Now the fifth one has gone."

In the evening, Deya Ali took the cattle home.

"Oh, Uncle," she said, "that stupid butter sat on a hot stone. She melted, and I've been looking after the cows on my own. I'm so tired and hungry."

"You must eat," said the lion, "then have a rest."

The next day, the lion said to Deya Ali, "Take the barley chaff out with you today."

So Deya Ali and the barley chaff took the cattle out. They guarded the cattle all day.

In the evening, Deya Ali said to the barley chaff, "We're hot and dirty. Let's go to the river and bathe."

"All right," said the barley chaff.

So they went to the river and bathed. The chaff tried to swim, but the water carried him away, one little piece after another.

"That's the end of the barley chaff," thought Deya Ali. "Now the sixth one has gone."

That evening, Deya Ali took the cattle home.

"That stupid barley chaff tried to swim in the river and floated away," she said to the lion.

"Who'll go with you tomorrow, then?" asked the lion.

"You must come with me, dear Uncle," said Deya Ali. "I can't go alone."

So the next day, Deya Ali and the lion went out together. At midday, Deya Ali made a big hole in the ground. She lit a fire inside it, and covered it with a cow-skin.

"Uncle, you're tired," she called out to the lion. "Come and rest."

The lion came and sat on the cowskin. At once it fell into the hole. The lion fell on top of it, and the fire burned him up.

Deya Ali danced and sang in triumph.

"I'm rich!" she shouted. "All the cows and goats and camels are mine!"

★★★

Not far away, some thieves were hiding in the bushes. They heard Deya Ali.

"Aha! Deya Ali is all alone now," they said to each other. "And nobody's helping her. Come on, brothers, this is our chance!"

When it was dark, the thieves came out of the bushes and surrounded the cattle pen. One tried to run off with a cow from one side. Another tried to grab a goat from the other side.

Deya Ali heard them. She began to run round the cattle pen fast, shouting loudly in different voices.

"Be careful, Uncle!" she cried. "The thieves are coming. Hey, brother, where's your stick? Mother, sisters, come quickly and help us!"

The thieves ran back into the bushes.

"Deya Ali isn't alone after all," they said. "Her family must have come to help her."

Deya Ali was very pleased with herself. She sat outside her hut and sang a song:

"The wicked thieves came
but they can't catch me!
I'm the wonderful,
clever Deya Ali!"

The next night, the thieves watched Deya Ali again.

"Tonight she really is alone," they said to each other. "Her family must have gone."

They waited until it was dark, and crept out

of the bushes again. Once again, they surrounded the cattle pen. One tried to run off with a cow. Another tried to grab a goat.

Deya Ali heard them. She snatched up some empty gourds and tied them to her waist, then she ran round and round the cattle pen. The gourds hit each other, and made a noise like this: *chellalum, chellalam, chellalum, chellalam!*

The thieves looked at each other.

"That sounds like horses!" they whispered.

Deya Ali called out, "Hey, Omer, your horse is too close. Move away! Idris! Ahmed! Don't go so fast! Your horse is touching mine!"

The thieves listened carefully.

"We know that voice," they said. "It's Deya Ali."

Deya Ali was running faster and faster.

Chellalum, chellalam, chellalum, chellalam, went the gourds.

"Osman! Abdi! Move away! Rein back! *Whoa,* there, boys!" Deya Ali was shouting.

The thieves smiled.

"That's only Deya Ali," they said. "There's nobody else with her at all. She's all by herself. Come on, brothers, the cows and goats and camels are ours!"

So the thieves ran up and took all the cows

and goats and camels. And when Deya Ali tried to stop them, they beat her with their sticks. At last they left her lying in the dust, all alone.

Deya Ali sat up when they had gone and looked around her. The cattle pen was empty. There were no cows or goats or camels in it now. The house she had once shared with her uncle and their friends was deserted too. No one would come and help her, bring her a drink or tend her bruises.

Deya Ali began to whimper.

"What a fool I've been!" she said to herself. "I wanted everything for myself and I couldn't bear to share it with my friends. Oh, my dear hyena, and vulture, and forked stick, and coffee beans, and butter gourd, and barley chaff, how I wish you were with me now! And my poor uncle! Why did I treat you so badly?"

She stood up and limped sadly back into the empty house.

"Friends are the greatest riches of all," she said. "I understand that now, and I'll never be greedy or selfish again."

The Sun and the Raven

Long, long ago, the Sun ruled in the sky. His name was Wak, and his messenger was the Raven.

The Raven used to fly from Wak the Sun down to the earth, and from the earth back up again, carrying messages in his beak. In those days, the Raven was white all over, with not a black feather on him. He bustled about, feeling important, and the other birds all looked up to him.

All was not well in the kingdom of the birds. They weren't happy together. The big birds usually ate meat, but sometimes they would rush in and snatch the seeds and fruit that the little birds liked to eat. Most of the time, the little birds were content to scratch on the ground for seed or to peck the fruit on the trees, but whenever they saw their chance they would dart in to grab a tasty morsel of meat from right under the big birds' beaks.

Things became worse and worse. Quarrels broke out every day. Feathers flew, and claws clashed.

"We can't go on like this," the birds all said to each other. "We must find a way to live together in peace. Let's find a judge who can advise us."

"The Raven! The Raven!" several birds called out. "He's Wak's messenger. Let's ask him."

The Raven agreed to help. He listened carefully as, one after the other, the birds put their points of view.

"This is a serious matter," he said at last, strutting up and down. "I must go and ask Wak for his opinion. And you must all agree to do whatever he says."

A babble of caws, tweets and hoots broke out.

"We agree! We agree!" chorused the birds.

The Raven flew off into the sky. He was away

for a long time, and when he came back, he called the birds together.

"Wak has spoken," he told them, puffing out his chest. "Listen to his wise words."

"We will," the birds all answered meekly.

"Wak has commanded that the big birds should eat only meat," the Raven said. "They should leave the fruit and seeds to the smaller birds, who must promise not to steal meat from the big ones."

"I agree," chirped the Finch, and all the little birds.

"So do I," croaked the Vulture, and all the big birds.

"But what about me?" squawked the Parrot. "Am I big or small? Where do I fit in?"

"And me?" cooed the Partridge.

"You must take me as your guide," said the Raven. "Anyone bigger than me should eat meat, and anyone smaller should eat seeds and fruit."

"Good advice," nodded all the birds, hopping up to measure themselves against the Raven.

"Wait a minute," chirped a smart little Roller Bird. "What about you, Raven? What are you allowed to eat?"

The Raven preened himself.

"I am the messenger of Wak," he said, "and I am a great sheikh, and can eat anything I like – seeds, fruit and meat, they're all allowed."

The other birds glared angrily at him.

"That's not fair!" they cried. "You've cheated us! We don't believe that Wak spoke to you at all."

They flew at him, their beaks snapping furiously.

The Raven was frightened. He shot up into the air, and, beating his wings as fast as he could, he flew up towards his master the sun.

"Wak!" he called out. "Help me! Wak! Wak!"

The birds were close behind him, their claws outstretched. Up and up flew the Raven, higher and higher. In his fear he flew too far, until he was close to the sun's fiery rays, and his white feathers were scorched to a sooty black.

From that day to this, the Raven has been black from beak to tail, and all the time he calls out, "*Wak!* Help me! *Wak! Wak!*"

The Good Prince

A great king once ruled the city of Harar.

He was blind. Doctors from far and wide had tried to cure him, but none of them could restore his sight. Tricksters and false magicians offered him remedies, but none of them worked, and they would run off quickly with the king's gold clinking in their pockets.

One day, a cunning fortune-teller told the king, "If Your Majesty captures the king of the seas, the Great Whale, and brings him here to your palace, he will make you see. I guarantee it. Oh yes, definitely."

"Capture the Great Whale?" cried the king. "No one could do such a thing."

"What about the prince, your son?" said the wily fortune-teller. "He's a fine fellow. Catching a whale would be nothing to him."

"My son! Of course! Send for him at once," said the king to his servants. "And pay this good, honest man handsomely. This scheme will work.

I feel it in my bones."

The prince, who liked to help everyone, agreed at once to his father's plan. He chose two of the king's soldiers to go with him, and together they went down to the sea. Then they set to work.

They tramped for miles along the beach, looking out to sea for the Great Whale's water-spout. They hired boats and sailed far and wide. They set traps, and cast nets, and whistled into the wind.

At last, all their efforts were rewarded, and the Great Whale, who was covered with gold from his shining nose to his gleaming tail, lay alongside the prince's boat in a huge net.

"Why did you catch me, Prince?" he said in his high, sing-song voice. "What do you want of me?"

The prince bowed respectfully. "Forgive me, sire," he said, "but I must take you to my father. Only you can cure his blindness and make him see."

The Great Whale lashed his golden tail, sending a big wave crashing over the bows of the boat.

"Oh, the folly of men!" he whistled. "Your father has been deceived by a greedy advisor. There's nothing I can do for him."

"Nothing?" said the prince, his heart sinking with disappointment. "But I promised my father that I would take you to his palace."

"If you do," said the Great Whale, "I will die. I can't live outside the sea. Let me go, Prince."

"So all my trouble has been for nothing," the prince said sadly, releasing the strings of the net, "and my poor father will never see again. But I have no wish to harm you. Excuse me, sire, for catching you."

"You're a noble young man," fluted the Great Whale, as he turned on a flipper and prepared to dive, "and I'm grateful to you for sparing my life. If you ever need my help, come to the shore and call for me. I'll do what I can to help you."

And in a shower of glittering spray, he had gone back down to the depths of his kingdom.

When the prince returned to the palace, his father called for him at once.

"Where's the Great Whale, boy?" he demanded.

"Bring him to me now."

The prince was afraid of his father's anger.

"I tried my best, Father, but I couldn't catch him," he said. "The Great Whale is the strongest creature in the sea. He escaped from me."

"I pinned all my hopes on you," cried the king. "Now I know that the beauties of the world will be hidden from my eyes for ever."

And he wept.

The two soldiers who had accompanied the prince nudged each other as they left the king's presence.

"That old king," the younger one said, "he's very free with his money. If we tell him what really happened, he's sure to reward us."

"I wouldn't want to get the young prince into trouble," the older one said. "He's a nice lad. He's been good to us too."

"Let's take a chance on it," the younger one said. "The king won't harm the prince. He's his only son."

But the soldier was wrong. When the king learned that the prince had caught the Great Whale and had let him go, he flew into such a furious rage that the pomegranates blew off the trees

in the royal garden, and the chickens in the courtyard jumped out of their feathers.

"You wicked boy! You deceived me!" he stormed at the prince. "From now on, you are no son of mine. Soldiers, where are you?"

"Here, sire," said the older soldier, stepping forwards unhappily.

"Take this traitor away and cut off his head," raged the king. "Throw his body to the dogs. His name will never be spoken in my presence again."

The two soldiers were filled with remorse.

"Oh sir, we never thought this would happen," the older one said to the prince, as he led him away in chains. "We're sorry, we really are."

"It was my fault," said the younger soldier, hitting himself on the head in shame. "Too greedy by half, I am."

"We won't let you come to harm," promised the older one. "We'll take you somewhere far from here, and let you go. We'll tell the king that we did the deed, but you'll not be harmed, never fear."

The soldiers did as they had promised. They took the prince to a distant land, and with many apologies, they said goodbye to him.

"What can I do now?" thought the prince. "Where can I go? I will have to travel the world alone."

Slowly, aimlessly, he walked on.

With a whisk of her tail and a toss of her head, an antelope suddenly leaped out in front of him. She skidded to a halt when she saw the prince.

"Oh sir, please help me," she panted. "The hunters are after me. They want to kill me!"

The prince's kind heart was touched.

"Come close," he said, "and bend your head down to my feet."

The antelope saw that she could trust the prince. She did as he asked, and the prince caught hold of one of her horns. A second later, the hunters came bursting out from the trees.

"That's our antelope!" they shouted. "We've been chasing her all day!"

"I'm sorry," the prince answered. "This one's

mine. But another antelope ran this way just a few minutes ago. That one must have been yours. He was much bigger and faster than this little thing. Look, that was the way he went, down towards the bottom of the hill."

The hunters didn't bother to answer, but took off at once, racing away in a spurt of dust, and as soon as they'd disappeared, the prince let go of the antelope's horns.

"You've saved my life," she said, a tear in her great brown eye. "One day, I will save yours. Call me if you need me, and I'll come and help you."

"How could an antelope ever help me?" thought the prince, but he thanked her politely and went on down the road.

He hadn't gone far, when a mouse darted out on to the path in front of him.

"Save me!" she squeaked. "Help me!"

The prince looked round and saw some boys hunting round on the ground. At once he took off his cloak, threw it over the mouse and sat down beside it.

The boys ran up to him.

"What are you doing, lads?" asked the prince.

"We're hunting a mouse," one of the boys

answered. "We want to have some fun with it."

"You've lost it, then," said the prince. "I saw it just now, but it bolted down a hole in the ground. You'll never find it now."

The boys went away, and the prince picked up his cloak. The mouse was still trembling from her whiskers to her tail, but she thanked the prince from the bottom of her heart.

"If ever you need help," she quavered at last, "call on me, and I'll come."

"How could a mouse ever help me?" thought the prince, but he thanked her politely and went on his way.

The prince travelled on and on, not knowing where he was going, crossing high mountains and swimming deep rivers. At last, one evening, worn out with hunger and fatigue, he looked up and saw in the distance a magnificent palace shining so brightly in the setting sun that his eyes were almost dazzled.

"Surely, in a place as lovely as that, someone will give me shelter for the night," he thought.

But when he reached the golden gates and tried to open them, he found that they were locked. He knocked again and again, and at last a doorkeeper opened them a crack and peered out.

"Who are you?" said the doorkeeper. "And what do you want?"

"I'm a poor man who is tired and hungry," said the prince. "Can you give me a bed for the night, and a little food and water? Surely a rich person must live in this house. Won't they let me in?"

The doorkeeper looked behind him nervously, then stepped out through the golden gates and whispered in the prince's ear, "Take my advice. Get away from here as fast as you can. Dozens of young men have come this way, but none have ever got out of here alive. My mistress is the most beautiful woman in the whole world, but she is possessed by an evil magic. Every man who sees her falls in love with her. She promises to marry them, but only if they pass a test. The test is impossible, and they all fail. And when they do, she kills them."

And pushing open the gate a little, he showed the prince a pile of bones lying just inside.

The prince felt his courage rise in his heart – and besides, he was filled with curiosity.

"The most beautiful woman in the world, you say?" he said slowly, and he thought to himself, "I must see her and take the test. After all, what is my life worth now?"

"Let me in, doorkeeper," he said bravely. "I'll take my chance like the rest."

"You poor young innocent," sighed the doorkeeper, stepping aside to let him in. "Well, I've done my best for you. There's none so foolish as those who won't be told."

The evil that possessed the mistress of the house had turned her into a great sorceress, and her magic was great and powerful. When the prince came into her presence, she was sitting on a golden chair in a golden room, and precious stones sparkled on the walls. But the prince saw none of them. He couldn't take his eyes off the sorceress who was, indeed, the most beautiful woman in the world.

"Marry me," he said.

The sorceress had seen countless young men stand before her. Usually, she waved her hand and commanded a servant to inform them of the test they had to take; but she had never before seen a young man as handsome as the prince, or one whose eyes were so full of goodness.

She laughed.

"Marry you? I don't even know your name," she said.

"It's the one thing I can't tell you," said the prince.

The sorceress was intrigued.

"I'll marry you," she said, "if you pass my test. Only then will my magic be broken. Hide yourself, stay hidden for three days, and on the fourth, come back to me. If I haven't been able to find you, I'll marry you. If I do find you, then you must die."

She had said these words many times before, but as she looked at the prince she felt sorry for the first time, and a little crack shivered through the evil in her heart.

"That's easy," said the prince, and her servants led him away and presented him with the finest supper he had ever eaten.

★★★

The next morning, as dawn broke, he was already hurrying down to the sea.

"Great Whale!" he called. "Come and help me!"

At once, a huge wave broke on the shore and out

of it appeared the head of the Great Whale.

"You promised to help me if ever I needed you," said the prince. "Hide me from the sorceress for three days, or she will kill me."

Without a word, the Great Whale opened his huge mouth and the prince stepped inside it. He felt his way down to the whale's vast stomach and hid beneath the massive ribs which soared above him in a high red vault.

For three days and nights the sorceress hunted for the prince. She flew over the mountains and scoured the valleys. She questioned the lions in their dens and the snakes in their holes, but she couldn't find the prince.

"No one has ever given me as much trouble as this," she thought, "but not even this man can hide from my magic telescope."

She put the telescope to her eye, and stared and stared, and at last, just as the third day ended, she spied the prince hiding in the whale's stomach.

As the sun set, the Great Whale swam back to the shore. He opened his mouth, and the prince walked down his tongue and stepped out on to the beach. He thanked the whale, and ran back to the sorceress's house.

"You didn't find me," he said, smiling joyfully. "So now you must marry me."

"But I did find you," said the sorceress. "You were hiding in the stomach of the Great Whale."

The prince's smile faded away, and he dropped his eyes.

"Then kill me," he said.

The sorceress's heart was stirred with pity, and another little crack ran through the hardness of her evil magic.

"No one has ever hidden as well as you," she said. "It was only by using my magic telescope that I could find you. I'll give you another chance. Go and hide again."

★★★

The prince ran out of the house as fast as he could. He went to a high place and called out, "Antelope! Come and help me!"

In a flash, the antelope stood before him.

"Hide me from the sorceress for three days," panted the prince, "or she will kill me."

"Follow me," said the antelope, and without another word, he turned and bounded up a steep mountain, and led the prince through a crack in the rock to a deep, dark cave.

For three days and nights the sorceress hunted for the prince. She dived to the depths of the sea, and floated up to the clouds. She questioned the turtles swimming through the waves and the eagles in their nests, but she couldn't find the prince.

"I've never had to look as hard as this," she thought, "but no one can hide from my magic telescope."

She put the telescope to her eye, and just as the third day ended, she saw the prince hiding in the antelope's cave.

"Here I am," the prince said happily, when he returned to the sorceress's house. "You didn't find me, I'm sure. Now you must…"

"But I did find you," interrupted the sorceress. "You did well, but my magic telescope did better. I saw you hiding in an antelope's cave."

"It's over then," said the prince. "Do what you must."

The sorceress wrung her hands. She didn't want to kill the prince. More tiny cracks were shivering through her stony heart.

"I will give you one more chance," she said at last, "but only one. Hide from me, but do it well, and if I can't find you, I promise I will marry you."

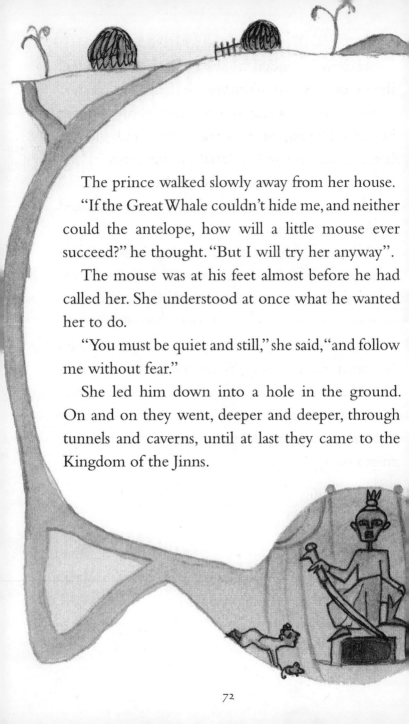

The prince walked slowly away from her house.

"If the Great Whale couldn't hide me, and neither could the antelope, how will a little mouse ever succeed?" he thought. "But I will try her anyway".

The mouse was at his feet almost before he had called her. She understood at once what he wanted her to do.

"You must be quiet and still," she said, "and follow me without fear."

She led him down into a hole in the ground. On and on they went, deeper and deeper, through tunnels and caverns, until at last they came to the Kingdom of the Jinns.

"Hide here, under the king's throne," whispered the mouse. "And don't move a whisker."

For three days the prince lay without stirring beneath the King of the Jinns' throne, and when at last he came back to the surface of the earth, he was pale and his eyes were dazzled by the light.

The sorceress was waiting for him. She looked more beautiful than ever.

"I searched for you in the burning deserts and on the snowy peaks," she said, "and I used my magic telescope until my eyes ached, but I couldn't find you anywhere."

As she spoke, the evil magic that had possessed her shivered into tiny pieces and fell away from her heart.

She married the prince the very next day, and they lived happily together for the rest of their lives.

Slippery Hirsi and Crooked Kabaalaf

Hirsi was a dishonest shopkeeper. He was as slippery as a bar of soap and as sly as a fox.

"Lock up your house when that rascal Hirsi's around," people warned their neighbours. "Let him in, and he'll have the lid off your cooking pot and the whiskers off your cat."

"And don't even think of buying anything from his shop," they said to one another. "He'd cheat his own mother if the poor woman was still alive."

Soon, everyone knew about Hirsi. No one would come into his shop any more, and every door in the town was barred against him.

Hirsi was disgusted.

"What a stupid place this is!" he thought. "People are so mistrustful. There's no room here for a man of my talents. I'll just have to go to the next town along the road and try my luck there. Now then, what do I have to sell?"

He looked round the room, and his eye fell on the fireplace.

"Hee-hee! I know. Ashes from my fire! I'll fill a sack with them and pretend it's flour. A fool is sure to buy it, and by the time he's taken it home and opened it up, I'll be safely back here with a purse full of money."

Some miles away, in the next town, there was another dishonest shopkeeper called Kabaalaf. He was as crooked as a jug-handle and as cunning as a monkey.

"Don't let that rogue Kabaalaf come inside your fence," everyone said. "He'll run off with the horns of your goats and the bridle of your donkey."

"And never buy anything from his store," they went on. "He'd snitch the cap from his own father's head, if the poor man wasn't already in his grave."

The whole town knew about Kabaalaf. People shook their heads disapprovingly when he went past, and told their children not to talk to him.

Kabaalaf was fed up with the place.

"I can't make a living here," he said to himself. "The people are such awful gossips. I suppose I'll have to go to another town and see how I get on. I must have something here that I can sell."

He looked out through his door and saw a flock of goats passing.

"Ho ho! The very thing! The goats' droppings are round and knobbly, just like coffee beans. I'll fill a sack with them and some idiot will buy it. Before he finds out, I'll be back home with the money jingling in my pocket."

And so, just as Hirsi was travelling down the road from east to west, with his sack full of ashes, Kabaalaf was on the very same road, going from west to east, with his sack full of goat droppings.

They met in the middle.

"Hm," thought Hirsi. "Here comes a fool. I'll try and sell my sack to him. It'll save me the bother of going any further."

"Aha," thought Kabaalaf. "Here comes a real bonehead. I'm sure I can sell him my coffee beans. Then I'll be able to go straight home."

"Good afternoon, stranger," said Hirsi, with a smile as wide as a crocodile's. "Are you going far?"

"Just to the next town," answered Kabaalaf, grinning like a hyena. "I have a sack of the best coffee to sell. It's yours for a good price, if you'd like to buy."

"Well, maybe," said Hirsi. "It so happens that I have some first-rate flour here that's looking for a buyer. I can give you a discount, if you'd care to take it."

Both men began to bargain, trying to beat each other down to the lowest possible price.

At last, Hirsi said, "I tell you what, my friend. Why don't we simply exchange sacks? I'll take your coffee beans and you can take my flour."

He could hardly stop himself laughing out loud, thinking of the beautiful coffee he'd have in exchange for a sack-load of ashes.

"Done!" cried Kabaalaf, almost exploding with mirth, as he thought of the excellent flour he'd have instead of a sack full of goat droppings.

So the two cheats exchanged sacks and hurried home.

When they opened their sacks, they were furious.

"Cheated! Me!" cried Hirsi. "I'll get my own back on that crook."

"I've been had!" roared Kabaalaf. "A beating's too good for that scoundrel."

As luck would have it, neighbours had overheard both the crooks, and the story of their double-crossing spread far and wide. Hirsi and Kabaalaf were laughed at so loudly that each of them decided to give up his crooked ways, and from that day they both became honest merchants.

The Miraculous Head

Now this is the strangest story you ever did hear, and it starts with a cross old man and his nagging wife, who gave birth to – a head. That's right. A head.

There was nothing wrong with the head. It had two eyes, two ears, a nose and a mouth, and was, in fact, a very fine head. But it was attached to nothing. The head had no arms, no legs and no body at all.

"Take it away, the nasty thing!" cried the woman to her husband. "I won't have it in the house! I'm sure it's all your fault, you stupid old man."

"How dare you blame me!" shouted her husband. "You're responsible for this."

And they began to quarrel bitterly in their usual way. The head watched his mother and father, and he sighed and rolled his eyes impatiently.

"A fine pair of parents I've got," he thought, but he said not a word.

When the old man and his wife had tired themselves out with quarrelling, the old man put the head into a sack, walked into town and left it by the side of the road.

The hours went past and the sun rose higher. It was hot and stuffy inside the sack. At last, the head heard two travellers pass by. He began to jump around, making the sack wriggle in a most peculiar way.

"Help! Get me out of here!" he yelled.

The travellers looked at each other.

"I'm not scared. Are you?" one of them said, trying to stop his voice trembling.

"Scared? Me?" said the other, trying to stop his knees knocking together.

"Help!" the head shouted again. "Don't be frightened. I won't hurt you!"

The travellers umm-ed and ah-ed, tiptoed backwards and forwards, urged each other on and plucked up their courage, until at last one of them dared to pick up the sack and open it. When they saw the head with no body, they were scared all over again, and nearly ran away.

"Don't be so silly!" the head said impatiently, and if he'd had a foot, he'd have stamped it. "How can I, a head, without arms or legs, possibly hurt you?"

"He's got a point there," the travellers said. "He can't possibly hurt us."

"Just take me to town and leave me at the nearest tea-shop," the head said. "And I won't trouble you any more."

So the travellers picked up the sack with the head rolling about inside it, and took it to the first tea-shop at the edge of town.

"Here's a present for you," they said to the tea-seller, and they ran away quickly before he'd had a chance to open the sack.

The tea-seller was shocked when he saw the head.

"What kind of wickedness is this?" he thought. "Some poor soul has had his head cut off, and those two villains must be the murderers. I'll take it out and bury it."

But as he lifted up the sack to carry it outside, the head called out, "Dear tea-seller, don't bury me. I have a question for you. Would you like to be rich?"

The tea-seller was so frightened to hear the head talking that his eyes opened wide until they were as round as oranges, and every hair on his head stood up straight.

"It's a d–devil! It's w–witchcraft!" he stammered. "The sooner I bury this cursed thing, the better."

The head sighed.

"Can't you answer a simple question?" he said. "I asked you if you'd like to be rich."

The tea-seller paused. He had always been a poor man, who had always worked hard for his living.

Perhaps, he thought, this thing isn't a devil after all, but a good fairy.

Aloud, he said, "Would I like to be rich? Well yes. Who wouldn't?"

"Then you're in luck," said the head. "Look after me, give me food and keep me safe, and soon, I promise you, you'll be rich."

The tea-seller, wondering what all this could be about, stood undecided while the steam hissed out of his kettle and a mouse ran across the floor.

"After all," he thought, "what have I got to lose? And it's only common decency to help when a poor soul asks, even if he doesn't have a body."

So from that day on, the head lived with the tea-seller and the tea-seller looked after the head. Every morning they shared their breakfast, and as they did so, the head gave the tea-seller his advice.

"The price of sugar's low in the market today," he would say. "Make sure you buy plenty. It's going to go up next week."

Or: "There are too many mice in here, tea-seller. They put the customers off. Sweep the place out. Make it nice and clean and tidy."

Or: "Put a new sign outside the tea shop. *Stop here for the best tea in town*. Travellers will see it as they come up the road, hot and thirsty, and they're sure to come in for a drink."

"You're right," the tea-seller would answer. "I should have thought of that myself."

New customers began to pour into the tea-shop.

"This is the best tea-shop in town," they said, and they came back, bringing their friends with them. Soon the tea-seller had enough money to add an extra room, and he even bought a donkey to carry his purchases back from the market.

Now, not far from the tea-shop was a great palace. The king lived in the palace with his only child. She was a girl of such beauty that birds fell out of the sky when they flew overhead, flowers turned on their stalks to watch her go past, and camels fell to their knees as she went by.

The customers in the tea-shop talked constantly about the princess. Hidden on a high shelf, where no one could see him, the head watched and listened.

"The man who marries that girl will be the happiest in the whole world," he overheard a customer say.

Another one shook his head.

"The king won't give her away that easily. Haven't you heard? Every man who comes to beg for her hand is asked for an impossible price."

"Such as?" asked the head softly.

The customers looked round, and assumed that one of them must have spoken.

"Well," one answered, "last week he told a young man to bring him a cat which could spin cloth."

"And the week before that," chimed in another, "he ordered a poor boy to fetch him a cow whose milk turns to gold when it touches the pail."

"The truth is," sighed a third, "that the king loves

his daughter too much. He doesn't want to give her to anyone at all."

"Oh, doesn't he?" thought the head. "We'll see about that."

The next morning, as the head and the tea-seller were eating their breakfast, the head said, "Tea-seller, have I been good to you? Have you grown rich, as I promised?"

"Oh yes, yes," nodded the tea-seller. "I'm very grateful. My business is now the best in town."

"Then do something for me," said the head. "Go to the palace and tell the king that your friend wants to marry his daughter. Ask him what sort of gift a suitor should bring."

The tea-seller looked pityingly at the head.

"The poor fellow doesn't know what he's talking about," he thought. "How could he possibly marry the king's daughter? Still, I might as well humour him. He's never asked a favour from me before."

So the tea-seller put on his best clothes and oiled his hair, and rubbed the dust off his sandals.

"Very smart," said the head, nodding his approval, and he settled down to wait for the tea-seller's return.

The tea-seller reached the palace and spoke

to the guard at the gate.

"My friend wants to marry the king's daughter," he said boldly, though he was quaking inside.

"Here's another fool," the guard called out over his shoulder. "Show him the way."

A servant led the tea-seller to the throne room. The king was sitting on his throne, interviewing suitors for his daughter.

The tea-seller's turn came at last.

"Excuse me, sire," he said, his voice squeaking nervously. "But my friend wants to marry your daughter."

"Why didn't he come himself?" yawned the king.

"He's – er – he's preparing his wedding clothes," said the tea-seller. "And please, sire, he'd like to know what present you require in exchange for your daughter's hand."

The king lazily brushed a fly off his nose with his horse-tail whisk.

"A camel would be a very fine thing," he said.

"A camel!" thought the tea-seller. "That's easy."

"A he-camel," the king went on, scratching his ear. "A very big and strong one with exceptionally good teeth."

"Oh ho!" thought the tea-seller. "There's nothing hard about that. He must like the look of me."

Aloud he said eagerly, "I'll bring you the finest camel in the world, sire. You'll have him by this time tomorrow," and he turned to hurry out of the throne room.

"Wait!" said the king, putting out a hand to examine his finger-nails. "When you bring this camel to my palace, it must speak to me in my own language and answer all my questions."

The tea-seller's face fell, and the servants standing around the throne room sniggered and nudged each other.

"What a fool!" they whispered. "Who does he think he is, anyway?"

"But, sire," the tea-seller was protesting. "A talking camel! That's impossible. How can a camel…"

But the king had already waved him away.

"Next!" he called out, and another suitor, dressed in his best clothes, with oil on his hair and clean sandals, was ushered into the throne room.

The tea-seller shook his head as he walked home.

"That was a lucky escape," he thought, with a shudder. "Whatever would the king have done if he'd accidentally betrothed his daughter to a head?"

The head was waiting impatiently for the tea-seller to return. He laughed triumphantly when he heard of the king's request.

"Nothing could be easier!" he exclaimed. "Let's go at once!"

"Go? Where?" said the tea-seller.

"To the camel market, of course. Where else will we find the beast we want?"

The tea-seller was beginning to lose patience.

"I've had enough of all this nonsense," he said crossly. "The tea-shop's been shut all morning, losing goodness knows how many customers, and now you want me to close down this afternoon as well. And for what? You know perfectly well that talking camels don't exist. The whole thing's ridiculous."

The head put on his most winning smile.

"Trust me, my dear friend. Just trust me. You'll never regret it, I promise you."

So, grumbling and mumbling, the tea-seller carried the head to the market, hiding him inside his sack, and together they inspected every camel in the market. There were big ones and small ones, crooked ones and straight ones, camels with

enormous humps and others with swishy tails. At last, the head hissed, "This is the one! We've found him! Pay the owner well, tea-seller, and take him to the palace, but leave me at home. It's not yet time for me to show myself."

As the tea-seller trudged back to the palace, leading the camel on a string, he muttered to himself, "A fine fool I'm going to look, trying to make this dumb brute speak, and all those sniffy servants will laugh at me again, I know they will."

When the king saw the camel being led into his throne room, he frowned a thunderous frown.

"What's this?" he roared. "Livestock in my quarters? Who's responsible for such an outrage?"

The servants standing round the room began to titter.

"Please, sir, I am," quavered the tea-seller. "You asked my friend to give you a camel, and here it is."

The servants began to laugh out loud.

The king remembered what he had said that morning.

"You stupid fellow! This is only a camel. It can't speak or answer questions. Do you think I'd give my beloved daughter away for the sake of an ordinary camel? Take this fellow away and whip him soundly."

The servants were laughing so hard, they could barely obey, but before they had time to march the tea-seller out of the throne room, the camel lifted its head and said, in a deep, growly voice, "Peace be upon you, O King."

Instantly the laughter died away. Everyone froze. The king started up from his throne.

"It's a trick," he said in a hoarse voice. "This camel can't really speak."

"Oh, but I can," said the camel. "And this good man has given me to you. I am yours now, O King, and you must give your daughter to this man's friend as you promised."

The king turned to the tea-seller.

"Who is your friend?" he demanded. "Why hasn't he come himself?"

The tea-seller, more shocked than anyone, was almost too terrified to stand.

"If you please, Your Majesty," he stammered, "he's a – he's a…"

Then he turned and fled in panic from the room.

"Bring your mysterious friend here tomorrow!" the king called out after him. "I'm a man of my word, and the wedding will take place, whoever the bridegroom turns out to be."

"You see what trouble you've brought upon us?" the tea-seller burst out, wringing his hands, when he told the head what had happened.

"Trouble? What do you mean? This is wonderful!" the head exclaimed. "My dear friend, I can never thank you enough."

"But what are we going to do?" wailed the tea-seller. "You can't possibly marry the princess!"

"Of course I can," smiled the head. "Didn't I tell you to trust me? Carry me to the palace tomorrow, and you'll see how it will all turn out."

All night long the poor tea-seller tossed and turned on his bed, imagining the rage of the king when he saw his son-in-law, and in the morning he could barely stand. The head, on the other hand, was in the best of moods, singing cheerfully to himself all the way to the palace.

The whole court was assembled to see the king's new son-in-law. The princess, dressed in her best clothes, was peeping shyly round from behind the throne, longing to catch a glimpse of him.

The king sighed with relief when he saw that the tea-seller had come on his own.

"This friend of yours," he said. "He's thought better of it. He doesn't want to marry my daughter after all. That's quite all right, my dear sir. There's no harm done. You can take your camel back and…"

"My friend is here," said the tea-seller, taking the head out of his sack and setting him down on a chair in front of the king.

At once, pandemonium broke out. The king snarled with helpless rage and struck his forehead in remorse. The queen screamed and fell into

a fit, drumming her heels on the floor. The princess stared at the head, her eyes round with horror. "No!" she whispered. "No! No!"

The head cleared his throat.

"It's going to speak," everyone whispered. "The thing speaks!"

"O King," said the head. "I gave you the gift you asked for, and I have come to marry your daughter."

"My poor, poor child," murmured the king. "But I gave my word, and I must keep it. I shall never forgive myself for my folly as long as I live."

The princess, who was as brave as she was beautiful, stepped forwards.

"It's all right, Father," she said. "What must be, must be."

And so the princess and the head were married, while the queen sobbed, and the king beat his chest with remorse, and the princess bit her lip and tried not to cry.

But as soon as the ceremony was over, there was a flash and a bang. When the smoke cleared, the head had disappeared, and there in its place was a handsome young man, tall and straight and sound in every limb, wearing noble dress.

The princess gasped with delight, and fell in love with him at once. The king stepped forward and gripped the young man's hand. The queen wiped her eyes and sent to the kitchens for a feast to be prepared.

That's nearly the end of the story. You just need to know that the king left the throne a year later, and gave his kingdom to his son-in-law. The tea-seller, helped by the new king, became the richest merchant in the country.

As for the cross old man and his nagging wife, they went on arguing for the rest of their lives and never knew what wonderful fate had befallen the son they'd thrown away.

ELIZABETH LAIRD is the author of *Red Sky in the Morning*, *The Garbage King* **and** *Crusade*, and has been shortlisted five times for the Carnegie Medal. She has travelled extensively throughout north-east Africa including Ethiopia, Kenya and the Somali regions, where she collected these stories from traditional storytellers. She met her husband while travelling on a plane in India, and they lived together in Iraq, Lebanon and Austria. Her first book for Frances Lincoln was *A Fistful of Pearls: Stories from Iraq*. Elizabeth divides her time between London and Edinburgh.